A LITTLE CRITTER® COLLECTION

GROWING EVERY DAY

BY MERCER MAYER

CHILDREN'S BOOK-OF-THE-MONTH CLUB
NEW YORK

GROWING EVERY DAY
A LITTLE CRITTER® COLLECTION

Just Go to Bed
Book, Characters, Text, and Images copyright © 1983 by Mercer Mayer

When I Get Bigger
Book, Characters, Text, and Images copyright © 1983 by Mercer Mayer

Just a Mess
Book, Characters, Text, and Images copyright © 1987 by Mercer Mayer

Just Going to the Dentist
Book, Characters, Text, and Images copyright © 1990 by Mercer Mayer

Just Lost!
Book, Characters, Text, and Images copyright © 1994 by Gina and Mercer Mayer

Just Me in the Tub
Book, Characters, Text, and Images copyright © 1994 by Gina and Mercer Mayer

This edition was especially created in 2002 for Children's Book-of-the-Month Club by arrangement with Random House, Inc. All rights reserved.

Printed in the United States of America

JUST GO TO BED

BY
MERCER MAYER

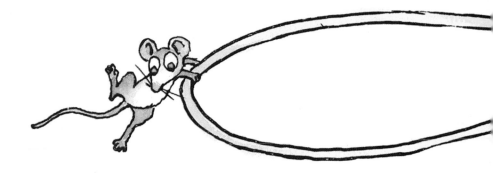

'm a cowboy and
I round up cows.
I can lasso anything.

Dad says…

"It's time for the cowboy
to come inside and get
ready for bed."

I'm a general and I have to stop the enemy army with my tank.

Dad says...

"It's time for the general to take a bath."

I'm a space cadet and I zoom
to the moon.

I capture a robot
with my ray gun.

Dad says…

"This giant robot has captured the space cadet and is going to put him in the bathtub right now."

Dad says, "It's time for the
sea monster to have a snack."

I'm a zookeeper feeding
my hungry animals.

Dad says…

"Feeding time is over. Here are the zookeeper's pajamas."

Dad says,
"The bandit chief
has caught you
so put on
your pajamas."

But I'm a race car driver
and I just speed away.

Dad says, "The race is over.
Now put on these pajamas
and go to bed."

I'm a bunny hopping around my garden.

Dad says…

"But I'm a bunny and bunnies don't sleep in a bed."

Mom says, "Shhh!"
Dad says, "Go to sleep."

Well, maybe a tired bunny
could sleep in a bed...

just this once.

WHEN I GET BIGGER

BY MERCER MAYER

When I get bigger
I'll be able to do
lots of things.

I'll go to the corner store by myself…

I'll wait until the light is green. Then I'll look both ways for cars before I cross the street.

I'll have my own watch and I'll tell everyone what time it is.

I'll go on a bus to Grandma and Grandpa's.

When I get bigger I'll have
a real leather football...

...my own radio, and a pair of
superpro roller skates.

I'll have a two-wheeler and a paper route.
I'll make lots of money.

At the playground
I'll help the little kids
on the swings.

I'll pick out
my own boots
at the shoe store.

I'll make a phone call
and dial it myself.

I'll order something
from a catalog…

…and it will come in
the mail.

When I get bigger I'll camp out in the backyard all night long.

Or I'll stay up to
see the end of the
late movie.
Even if I get sleepy,
I won't go to bed.

But right now I have to go to bed...

…because Mom and Dad say…

...I'm not bigger yet.

JUST A MESS

BY
MERCER MAYER

Today I couldn't find my baseball mitt.

I looked in my tree house.

I looked under the back steps.

I asked Mom if she had seen it.
She said I should try my room.

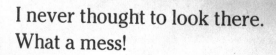

I never thought to look there.
What a mess!

RINGO

A
FUN
GAME

Mom said it was time
to clean my room.
So I asked her to help.

She said, "You made the mess,
so you can clean up the mess."

Dad was working in the yard.
He said he was too busy to help me.

My little sister said, "No way!"
And the baby didn't understand.

I just did it myself.

First, I put a few things in the closet.

I put my clothes
in the drawers.

I straightened up
my games.

I shut the lid
to my toy box

and put away my books.

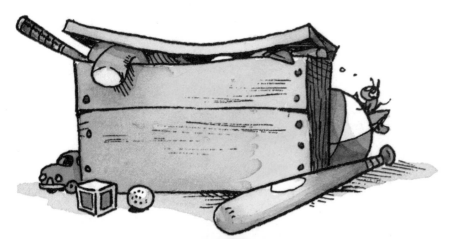

The rest of the mess could fit under my bed,
so I put it there.

Then I made the bed.
Won't Mom be pleased.

I thought I might wash the floor.

But Mom said, "NO!"
So I just vacuumed instead.

Everything was just about perfect.

Then I noticed that my pillow was missing.

I looked on the other side of my bed,

and guess what I found?

My baseball mitt.

JUST GOING TO THE DENTIST

BY
MERCER MAYER

For Len, Jessie,
Arden & Benjamin
My Wonderful Children
who have and will make
our dentist rich.

Mom took me to the dentist.
She said I needed a checkup.

DR. GHUM

DENTIST
FOR
SMALL CRITTERS

I didn't need a checkup.
My teeth were just fine.
But we went anyway.

At the dentist's office we met the nurse.
She gave us a great big smile.
I think she was showing off her teeth.

The dentist wasn't ready to see me,
so we sat in the waiting room.

CRITTER
FASHIONS

Other kids were there, too.
One of the bigger kids had wires
all over her teeth.
Mom said they were braces.
I thought they were neat.
I hoped I would get braces.

We had to wait a long time but there were toys to play with…

…and books to read.

When it was my turn, the nurse
came to get me.

I had to see the dentist all by myself.
But I didn't mind — too much.

We went into a really weird room.
It looked like a spaceship.

I sat in a funny chair.
It was called a dentist chair.
The nurse put a bib on me.

Then the nurse said that she
was going to clean my teeth.
It tickled a lot.

She told me to spit in the sink.
No grown-up had ever asked me to
spit before.
That was cool!

Next she took pictures of my teeth.
They were called X-rays.
Just like Super Critter's
X-ray vision.

Then the dentist came in.
He looked inside my mouth with
a little mirror on a stick.

The pictures of my teeth were ready.
So the dentist called in my mom and we
all looked at the pictures of my teeth.

FALSE TEETH
FOR A TIGER

The dentist said I had one cavity
and that he could fix it right then.

They put me back in the dentist chair.
The dentist told me he was going to give
me something so I wouldn't feel anything.

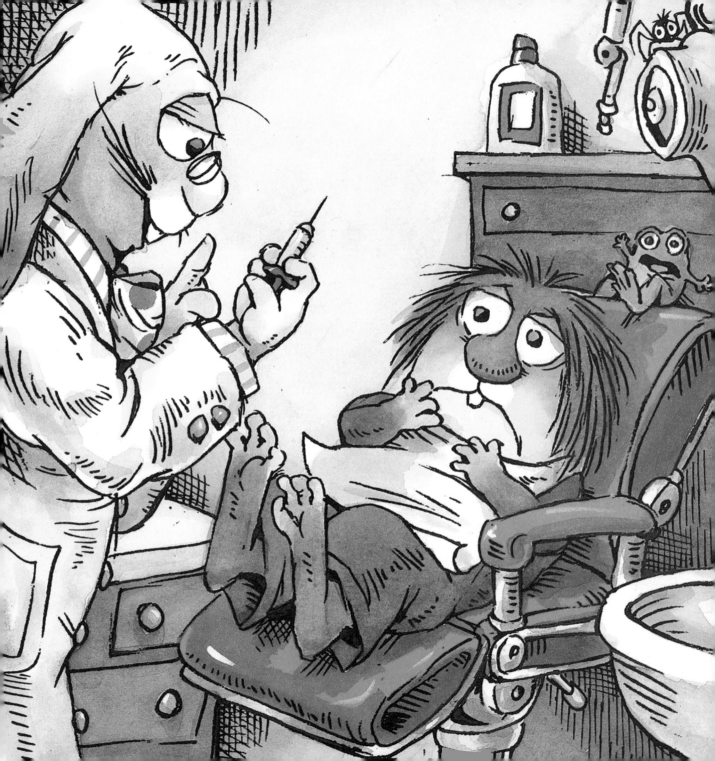

I closed my eyes real tight
and counted to ten.

Before I knew it, the dentist said
it was all over.
I hardly felt anything.

Yuck, then my mouth went numb.
It was weird; I couldn't feel my tongue.

Then the dentist said he was going
to drill a hole in my tooth and clean
out my cavity.
There was a lot of noise in my mouth.
But it didn't hurt.

BUZZZZZZZ

When the dentist finished,
he sent me out to my mom.
The nurse gave me a treat for free.

You know, going to the dentist
wasn't so bad.
It just made me tired.

JUST LOST!

BY GINA AND MERCER MAYER

For Matthew &
Lauren Atkinson

Mom took us shopping at the mall. There were a jillion critters there.

I wanted to push my brother's stroller,
but the mall was just too crowded.
Mom pushed him instead.

There was such a big crowd that I could barely see anything. Mom said, "Stay close by me so you won't get lost."

When we were right in the middle of the
crowd, I noticed that my shoe was untied.
I tied it so I wouldn't trip.

When I stood up, I couldn't find Mom.
I climbed up on a bench to look around.

I yelled, "MOM!"
But it was so noisy,
no one could hear me.

My mom was lost at the mall!

I wanted to cry, but I didn't.
I was brave instead.

The store clerk said, "May I help you?"
I said, "My mom is lost!"

She said, "Don't worry,
we'll find her for you."
She called a security guard
on the store phone.

The clerk let me play with
some toys while we waited
for the security guard to arrive.

The security guard was wearing
a uniform. He looked like a policeman.
"You can come to my office until
we find your mom," he said.

He let me wear his hat.

I felt really cool walking through the mall with a security guard.

The security office was a small room.
There were lots of TV sets showing
everything at the mall.

I saw a critter crying.
I guess she didn't want
to leave the toy store.

I saw critters reading
in the bookstore.

I saw critters eating
in the restaurants.

But none of them could see me.
It was like being a real spy.

The security guard made an announcement over the loudspeaker: "Little Critter's mom, please come to the security office to pick him up."

Then he gave me a doughnut and some juice. He let me look through the Lost and Found box.

All of a sudden I saw my mom on one of the TV screens. She was walking through the mall with another security guard. I said, "There she is—that's my mom!"

The office door opened.
Mom and my brother and sister came in.

Mom looked worried. I guess she's just not
as brave as me. She said, "I was so worried."
I said, "I was really brave. I didn't even cry."
Then Mom smiled and said, "I'm very
proud of you, Little Critter."
I knew she was glad
I found them.

The next time we go to the mall
I'm going to be really careful.
Mom just hates getting lost at the mall.

JUST ME IN
THE TUB

BY GINA AND MERCER MAYER

For Lauren Atkinson

When I take a bath, there are lots of things that I have to do.

First I start to run the water in the tub.
I like it to be nice and warm.
Sometimes it takes a little while to
get the water just right.

Then I put in the bubble stuff. I have to be careful not to pour in too much.

While the water is running, I get my towel
and washcloth. I like big fluffy towels.

I get my pajamas, too.
I always look for clean ones.

Then I take off my clothes and get into the tub.

When the water is just deep enough,
I turn it off. If I let the water run too much,
it could splash on the floor.

I always wash before
I play in my bath.

I start with my face . . .

then I wash my hair . . .

and my feet . . .

Then it's time to play with my toys.
If I forget something, I never bother
Mom—I just go and get it.

I can't take my stuffed animals into the tub. But I bring them into the bathroom, so they won't feel left out.

I like to play with my pirate ship
in the tub. Sometimes my pirate ship
is caught in a terrible storm and ends up
stranded on a desert island.

I have pots and pans to play
with in the tub, too. I like to
make bubble cakes. But
they don't taste too good.

I can make myself
look like Santa Claus.

I play in the tub until my mom says, "Time to come out now!"

I knew it was time because
the water was getting cold.

When I get out of the tub,
I step on the bath mat, so I
won't splash water everywhere.

Sometimes Mom comes in
and helps me dry off.

Then I put on my nice clean pajamas.

I always remember to let
the water drain out of the tub.
But sometimes I forget
about my toys.

Then I wipe up the
floor, just in case
I splashed a little.

And I put my
dirty clothes
in the basket.

Taking a bath can be a real job.

But it always makes me
feel warm and cozy.